ERNI CABAT'S MAGICAL WORLD OF

COBBLEHILL BOOKS   Dutton/New York

MONSTERS

Paintings by **ERNI CABAT**

Text by **DANIEL COHEN**

Library of Congress Cataloging-in-Publication Data
Cabat, Erni.
[Magical world of monsters]
Erni Cabat's magical world of monsters / paintings by Erni Cabat ; text by Daniel Cohen.
p.   cm.
Summary: Depicts such legendary monsters as the dragon, griffin, and chimera and discusses what
was known or believed about them.
ISBN 0-525-65087-3
1. Monsters—Juvenile literature.   2. Animals, Mythical—Juvenile literature. [1. Monsters. 2. Animals,
Mythical.]   I. Cohen, Daniel, date.   II. Title.   III. Title: Magical world of monsters.
GR825.C27 1992   398.24'54—dc20   91-34241   CIP   AC

Published in the United States by Cobblehill Books, an affiliate of Dutton Children's Books, a division
of Penguin Books USA Inc.

Designed by Jean Krulis

Printed in Hong Kong
First Edition 10   9   8   7   6   5   4   3   2   1

INTRODUCTION

Somewhere in a misty realm between what we know and what we believe is the land of monsters. These creatures, usually terrifying and always strange, have haunted our imaginations for thousands of years. We're not talking about monsters out of books or movies, creatures that somebody made up to scare us. We're talking about monsters that people really believed in, and perhaps still believe in.

Here are fantastic creatures that steal and guard treasure, that can kill with a breath or a glance, that can sink ships with their tentacles, or set fire to a kingdom. Where did stories of these remarkable beasts begin? Why were they believed in for so long? What manner of creatures were they? And what did they look like?

Join us now for a journey into the land of monsters.

DRAGON

Of all the world's monsters, this one is king. Ancient Romans, Medieval knights, and Chinese emperors all believed in Dragons. To the Romans, the Dragon was a gigantic snake. By the Middle Ages, it had acquired legs, wings, and the ability to breathe fire. It ravaged the countryside, stole treasures, and was a symbol of evil.

The Dragon of China and Japan may have looked like the Western Dragon, but it had a very different character. It was a symbol of royalty and good luck. Those fortunate enough to meet an Oriental Dragon went away with a generous gift.

A few hundred years ago in Europe, when people found bones of long-extinct mammals like the woolly rhinoceros, they would identify them as the bones of Dragons. It was assumed that Dragons lived in underground caves and almost never came to the surface. In China, many fossils were also believed to be Dragon bones. The Chinese would grind them up and use them as medicine.

GRIFFIN

A gigantic beast, half lion and half eagle, that loved gold and precious stones, the Griffin roamed the mountains of Central Asia in search of treasure. When he found it, he would take the treasure back to his lair and stare at it for hours, hypnotized by the reflected gleam of sunlight and moonlight.

The Romans heard rumors of Griffins and how fierce they were. It was said that when a Griffin settled in an area, the humans had to flee. One ancient writer warned people to stay away from Griffins "because it feasts on them at every opportunity." The warning continued, "It is also extremely fond of eating horses."

The claws of the Griffin were believed to possess magical powers. Cups made from the claws of a Griffin were highly prized. Such a cup would change color if poison was put into it. Sometimes merchants would bring what they called Griffins' claws to the markets of Medieval Europe. These were usually the tusks of extinct mammoths and mastodons.

CHIMERA

This is the most fantastic of all monsters. Even the Greeks, who originated the idea of the Chimera, were not quite sure what it looked like. She—for there was only one Chimera, and it was female—was part lion, part goat, and part serpent. Just how the different parts were arranged depended on who was describing the creature. The Chimera was extremely fierce and dangerous. She belched smoke and flame wherever she went.

The monster had taken up residence on a mountain in the Kingdom of Lycia. The whole region had been burned and blackened by her flames. Only birds could live there because they could fly above the Chimera's fire.

The hero Bellerophon decided to challenge the monster. He had already tamed the winged horse Pegasus, so he was able to fly over the land.

Bellerophon had a plan. He carried a load of lead. When the Chimera reared up and began breathing flames, Bellerophon dropped the lead into its mouth. The flames melted the lead and choked the creature.

BASILISK

The name Basilisk comes from the Greek and means "little king." To the ancients, the Basilisk was king of the snakes. It was described as a snake with a crownlike structure on its head. As time went on, it acquired a more elaborate and more terrifying reputation. By the Middle Ages, the Basilisk had become the most feared and most deadly of monsters. It was so noxious that the mere presence of a Basilisk would make birds fall down out of the sky, cause fruit to rot, and streams to become poisoned and dry up. The glance of a Basilisk could kill any other living thing, including itself. When people went Basilisk hunting, they carried a shield polished like a mirror. The idea was to have the creature see its own reflection and die.

According to one version of the Basilisk legend, the creature was born from an egg laid by a rooster and hatched by a toad. Instead of a snake with a crown, the Basilisk had been transformed into a creature that had the characteristics of a snake, rooster, toad and, occasionally, lizard.

KRAKEN

One monster of legend turned out to be real. For centuries there had been tales of a horrifying sea creature called the Kraken. It was said to look like an uprooted tree, with eyes larger than dinner plates and a beaklike mouth. This monster would rise up out of the water and entangle entire ships in its tentacles.

As recently as two hundred years ago, sailors would return from voyages with tales of the Kraken. There were even rumors that the remains of such creatures had been found washed up on remote beaches. A few noted that the Kraken sounded like a giant version of the squid. But the only squids people knew about were quite small.

Most people assumed that the squid didn't grow much more than a foot in length. And most people were wrong. During the 1870s, several really gigantic squids were washed ashore. The largest was fifty-five feet long from the tip of its tail to the tip of its longest tentacle. Squids do not attack ships, but they are quite large enough to have inspired the legend of the Kraken.

CERBERUS

Cerberus is a many-headed dog who, in the myths of the ancient Greeks, guarded the gate to the gloomy Underworld where the spirits of the dead were sent. It was Cerberus' task to nip at the heels of souls unwilling to enter the dreaded realm, and to eat the spirits of those who try to leave.

Cerberus was so vicious that he was considered the greatest challenge to the hero Hercules. The last and hardest of the twelve labors set for the hero by King Eurystheus was to bring the monster dog back from the Underworld. The king hoped that Hercules would be killed in the attempt.

Hercules marched right into the throne room of Hades, ruler of the Underworld, and demanded Cerberus from the god. Hades told him he could have him if he could capture him without the use of clubs or arrows.

Hercules went to where Cerberus was chained, jumped on the monster's back, and choked him into submission. The hero then took the animal to the upper regions and showed him to King Eurystheus. The king was so startled that when Cerberus snarled at him, he died of fright. Hercules then returned Cerberus to the Underworld.

MEDUSA

Medusa, whose hair was a mass of living snakes, is the most famous of the monsters called Gorgons. Sometimes artists have showed Medusa as an ordinary-looking and even a beautiful woman—if you could overlook those snakes. To the ancient Greeks, however, the Gorgons were truly monstrous. They had broad, flat faces, large mouths with fangs, and their tongues lolled out. They were right out of your worst nightmare.

Next to the snakes, what everyone remembers about the Gorgons is that anyone who looked at one immediately turned to stone. Some said it was the magical power of their eyes. Others believed the faces were so terrible that people froze at the sight.

The hero Perseus was sent by a king—who hoped that the youth would never return—to bring back the head of the Gorgon, Medusa. Perseus knew he couldn't look directly at Medusa. So he brought along a mirror. At the right moment, he turned his back on the monster, looked into the mirror and, wielding his sword backward, was able to cut off her head.

CENTAUR

When the horse was first domesticated, it was used to pull carts and later, chariots. The Greeks had used chariots and cart horses, but had never seen anyone riding a horse until they met the Scythians who lived north of the Black Sea. These wild horsemen not only rode on the backs of horses but, while mounted, were able to shoot arrows with deadly accuracy. Horse and rider seemed almost like a single creature. Stories of these horsemen formed the basis of the legend of the Centaur.

The Centaur of Greek myth had the upper torso of a man and the body of a horse. There were no female Centaurs. These horselike creatures were the symbol of barbarism. They ate raw meat, and were driven mad by wine, which turned them into raging killers with slashing hooves and clawing hands.

One was different. His name was Chiron, and he was skilled in the arts of healing, hunting, and music. When Chiron died, the god Zeus sent his great body into the sky as the constellation Sagittarius, the archer.

MINOTAUR

The ancient Greeks told the story of the Minotaur. This was a monster with the head of a bull, the body of a man, and the temper of a mad killer. The creature was kept by Minos, king of the island of Crete. The monster lived in a building with so many rooms and corridors that once you got in, you could never get out. It was called the labyrinth.

Every year Minos would send his ships to the Greek City of Athens. He would demand seven Athenian boys and seven girls, who would be thrown into the labyrinth for the Minotaur. The Athenian hero Theseus offered himself as a sacrifice. When Theseus entered the labyrinth, he was able to kill the monster and find his way out.

Just a legend? When archaeologists began digging up the ruins of ancient Crete, they found a huge building. It was a mass of rooms and corridors. The story of the labyrinth immediately came to mind. Everywhere there were images of bulls.

HYDRA

In the list of many-headed monsters, this is the champ. In some accounts, the Hydra had a mere seven or nine heads. In others, it had a hundred or more. It was hard to kill because every time one of the heads was cut off, two new ones would grow in its place. The hero Hercules figured out a way. He set fire to the forest around the monster's lair. Then he used flaming logs to burn off the monster's heads, so that they could not grow back.

The myth of the Hydra was probably inspired by the many-armed octopus or squid. In some of the earliest accounts, the Hydra was supposed to live in or near the water.

Though stories of the Hydra seem obviously fantastic, people continued to believe in the creature. What were said to be preserved Hydras were displayed all over Europe for many centuries. People who saw them thought they were real. A famous one in Hamburg, Germany, was made of a snakeskin, weasels' heads and paws. To people who believed that a multiheaded monster was possible, it seemed perfectly realistic.

PHOENIX

About two thousand years ago, a Greek traveler named Herodotus went to Egypt. He was told many strange tales. Some he believed, some he did not. One of the stories was of a bird called the Phoenix. "I have never seen the Phoenix myself, except in paintings," he said. Still, he reported what he had heard. The bird was the size and shape of an eagle. Its plumage was partly red and partly gold. One story said that the Phoenix lived for five hundred years. When it died, its offspring carried it from Arabia to Egypt to bury it near the Temple of the Sun.

There was an even more fabulous Phoenix legend. When the bird sensed its own approaching death, it would build a funeral pyre and throw itself into the flames. Nine days afterward, the bird would be reborn from its own ashes. Some believe the Phoenix was a symbol for the sun. The sun seems to die in its own fires every night, and then rise again the next morning.